20

Skylark

For Pat and David

Skylark

K. M. PEYTON

Illustrated by Liz Roberts

Oxford University Press

Oxford   Toronto   Melbourne

Oxford University Press, Walton Street, Oxford OX2 6DP
Oxford New York Toronto
Delhi Bombay Calcutta Madras Karachi
Petaling Jaya Singapore Hong Kong Tokyo
Nairobi Dar es Salaam Cape Town
Melbourne Auckland

and associated companies in
Berlin Ibadan

OXFORD is a trade mark of Oxford University Press

British Library Cataloguing in Publication Data
Peyton, K. M.
Skylark
I. Title. II. Roberts, Liz
823'.914[F]

ISBN 0-19-271584-4

Set by Pentacor Ltd, High Wycombe, Bucks
Printed in Great Britain

1

Ben knew there was somebody there right from the beginning—a footprint in the brown leaf-mould, the faintly trodden path between the garden door and the spring pool . . . a 'feel' of somebody . . . once, in the evening, a faint blue spiral of smoke out of the broken trees.

'Somebody lives down there,' he said, looking out of his bedroom window.

'I bet,' said Mitzi.

'Somebody lives in the trees. With a cat, and hens.'

He had seen the cat, and heard a hen.

'Your stories!'

'We could go and see. Tomorrow.'

'Catch me!'

Mitzi wore high heels and rocked and stumbled round the house, and only went outside as far as the door of the Mini in the yard. She had a bright red mouth and bright yellow hair in a frizz. Ben's mother hired her to look after Ben. She was called a Help. Ben thought a help was something you shouted when you were drowning or being chased by a bull, but apparently not . . . a help was Mitzi. They lived together in a big lonely house down a long drive, a long way from anywhere.

'Come and see with me,' he said again. He was too frightened to go on his own.

'See where?'

'Over the gap in the wall, in the wood.'

Mitzi laughed. 'What, me? There's no paths in there.'

Ben scowled. He never had anyone to do anything with, because there wasn't anyone but Mitzi and she had what she called sniffily 'Other Interests'. This seemed to be lying about reading romantic novels, listening to pop records and watching television. She was looking after him until his mother came back, which was supposed to be soon, but wasn't very.

If there was someone living in the wood—and Ben was quite sure that there was, from all the signs—it must be someone quite interesting. You

2

would have to be interesting to live in a wood secretly. Ben was dying to have an interesting friend to talk to. A gypsy perhaps . . . At the moment there was only George, who came twice a day to feed the young bulls in the stockyard next to the house. The house had once been the farmer's, but the farmer had built himself a smart new one on the road and let the old house to Ben's mother, although he still used all the buildings.

George called Ben 'Skylark', because whenever Ben went outside Mitzi buckled him into a life-jacket, in case he fell into the spring pool or, if he went further, into the canal. She had bought the life-jacket for 5p in a jumble sale and it was rather large for him and had SKYLARK painted on each side in faded letters. Ben didn't like it, it made him so fat. But Mitzi was adamant.

'I'm adamant,' she said, barring the door to him, holding up the life-jacket.

Ben considered.

'What's "adamant" mean?'

'It means I mean it.'

She wasn't adamant about much, so Ben reckoned it wasn't worth arguing about.

Except for George coming to the stockyard, Ben had all the outside to himself. Outside was far the best: the yard, and beyond it the walled garden with the spring pool in it and the overgrown orchard and the jungle beyond that and all the fields down to the canal. It was all his own territory. Or was it?

In a patch of mud on the edge of the spring pool was a footstep. It wasn't his. It was too big. But too small to be George's. And across the grass was a faint trail, as if someone walked up that way quite often. To the spring pool. Ben followed it the other way across what had once been a lawn. At the bottom the trees had taken over—some of them had fallen across the wall and broken it down, and the loose bricks had become overgrown with ivy. There was a door in the wall that led into the wood, but it was shut fast and immovable.

Ben climbed up over the ivy on to the top of the broken part and sat for a bit, looking and listening. It was a little bit scary, thinking there was somebody there, somebody who shouldn't be. He didn't want to go any further, just in case. It might be a murderer, holing up from the police, or a terrorist. With small feet.

Ben sniffed. He could smell, faintly, wood-smoke. But there was no bonfire anywhere. And bacon.

Bacon?

'Yes. Definitely bacon,' he said out loud. He often talked out loud.

He knew he had to find out about the bacon, but did not feel very brave about going on into the wood. He needed somebody with him. In the garden, under an old pear tree, there was a little tombstone all covered in nettles, and on it was engraved: 'Oscar. A brave dog. 1929–1938.' Ben had cleared away the nettles as best he could and put beside the stone a jam jar of plastic roses, which he had found in the dustbin. Ben always wished Oscar was real. He used to pretend quite often that Oscar was with him. He saw him as a sort of spaniel, brown and white, and chunky. And brave. Oscar must have known the wood, and seen off all manner of tramps and gypsies.

Ben got cautiously off the wall into the wood, and proceeded very nervously—Oscar or no Oscar—into its fringes. His heart was beating very thumpily. He had never been right into the wood. It was very creepy, sometimes totally silent, sometimes creaking and rustling in the wind in a very lively fashion. The trouble was, once you were well in, you had no idea of which way to go, and quite soon forgot which way the house was, there being no paths or tracks. You could only get through at all because a lot of the elm had died, and there were clearings and thin bits. Ben wouldn't go further than he could see the sky back above the garden. He didn't want to get lost in there with a terrorist or a murderer.

The smell of bacon was stronger. He stopped and

listened. Silence. Dead, creepy silence. A thin blue suggestion of wood-smoke veiled the dead brown trees.

'Oscar!' he called loudly, to prove he was brave too.

But his voice was shaky, and before the call had faded he had turned round and was going back, more quickly than he had come. He could not help feeling terribly relieved to be back on the wall and looking down into the familiar, safe garden.

'There is someone there,' he said.

He went and stood by Oscar's grave for a bit, wishing he had a live Oscar to explore with. Mitzi was always going on about being lonely, but Ben didn't understand what lonely was, because he didn't know anything else. He looked at the date and tried to work out how old Oscar would be now. He was good at numbers. It came out at about sixty. A jolly old dog.

Then he went back and looked at the footprint by the spring pool.

'Whoever it is, must come and get water here.'

It made sense. If you didn't want to be seen you would come at night, or very early in the morning. If he kept watch out of his bedroom window he would see whoever it was. He could solve the mystery quite easily, without having to be brave at all.

6

He was very pleased with this idea. He stood looking at the spring pool. Emma, the wild duck who lived there, came to see if he had any bread, but he hadn't. Emma was twelve years old, according to George. She slept cleverly in the middle of the pool with her head tucked under her wing so the foxes wouldn't catch her. Ben wondered why she didn't get cold. The water was icy. It bubbled up out of the ground on the far side and came into the pool which had been especially made for it, lined with gravel, quite deep. It had lacy weeds swimming in it, and minnows.

Ben went back indoors and took off Skylark and waited to go to bed, so that he could spy on the maker of the footprint.

Mitzi was amazed when he offered to go to bed early. It didn't get dark till gone ten o'clock, so as soon as he was in his bedroom and the door shut, and Mitzi had departed to watch television, he settled down by the window to watch the spring pool. He watched resolutely till dark came but nobody appeared.

He decided that early morning would be a more likely time and decided to watch from dawn, but after his late-night vigil it was two more nights before he managed to wake up in time for dawn.

Even then it was dawn quite well on, the room light and the birds singing hard. Ben got out of bed quickly and ran to the window. It was freezing cold and the garden was all glittery and sharp and wet-looking, the shadows long and spiky across the grass. Two rabbits were washing their faces by Oscar's grave and a green woodpecker was spiking holes in the grass like Mitzi's heels. Everything was in order.

Ben looked for a bit, then got cold and fetched his dressing-gown. He was half-inclined to go back to bed, but decided to man the lookout like a proper scout. How could he find out who was frying bacon if he couldn't keep watch for even ten minutes? Dawn would soon be gone and George came quite early. Whoever it was would come before George. Perhaps had already been and gone.

He pulled up a chair and sat in the window, watching.

Just as he was beginning to get very very bored, he saw something move at the far end of the jungly garden. Somebody climbed up on to the wall where it was broken down and sat there, looking in his direction.

It was a *girl*!

Ben stared, now very much awake—in fact his heart started to thump like it had in the wood, although there was no reason now. The girl couldn't possibly see him, as he was half-behind the curtains and low down. She was carrying a bucket

and, as he watched, she jumped down and came up
the garden to the spring pool. Emma woke up and
swam towards her as if she was used to the visit,
and the girl pulled some bread out of her jeans

pocket and threw it to her. While she was eating,
the girl filled the bucket with water. She was in no
hurry and did not seem at all nervous.

She was a stocky, four-square sort of girl, with
black curly hair, quite long, and a rather cross-
looking face. She wore old jeans and a navy-blue
jersey.

She squatted down and fed some bread to Emma
out of her hand, which made Ben cross because he
had never managed to get Emma to feed out of his
hand, although he had tried. Then she stood up and
went back the way she had come, carrying the
bucket of water. She climbed over the wall with it
in a very practised fashion, as if she had been doing
it every day for weeks. As no doubt she had. Then
she was gone.

Ben sat on his bed thinking. He knew he had to
speak to the girl, which meant following the wood-
smoke/bacon smell into the wood and accosting
her. It was his wood, after all.

But suppose . . . and she had had rather a fierce
face. What if she . . . ? Well, what if she what?
What could she do, save talk back to him? She
didn't, to be honest, look like either a murderer or a
terrorist.

'I'll do it tomorrow,' Ben thought. He had done
quite enough for one day.

But, if he were honest, he knew he only said

tomorrow because he was frightened of facing the girl. The more he thought about it, the more he realized that the longer he thought about it the more nervous he would get.

He compromised.

'I'll go this afternoon. With Oscar.'

Mitzi was going to make marmalade after lunch. That would keep her quiet.

'You must keep out of my way,' she said. 'I have to concentrate.'

That suited Ben very well. Mitzi usually spent all day playing records after she had cleared up, and being very mopy, saying she was lonely and wishing she could get away. 'If I had a thousand pounds,' she kept saying, 'if I had a thousand pounds, you wouldn't see me for dust. It's like being in solitary confinement, living here.'

'What's solitary confinement?' Ben asked.

'It's being shut up in prison all by yourself.'

'You aren't all by yourself. There's me. And you're not shut up. If you don't like it you can go,' he said bravely, wondering whatever would happen to him if she did.

'I can't go, any more than you can.'

'I don't want to go.'

'That's the difference. Lucky old you.'

'Why can't you go?'

'There's a thing called money, and a roof over

your head and something to eat . . . if I had a thousand pounds now . . .'

This conversation took place fairly often, so when Mitzi decided she was going to make marmalade, Ben thought, splendid, that would keep her nice and occupied. So as soon as Mitzi had cleared away and got out her oranges, Ben put on Skylark and went outside.

2

It was a soft, warm afternoon, without wind. Ben walked down to the broken bit of wall and climbed up and sat on the top. No smells, no sound, nothing. He was rather trembly. Oscar wasn't really much good, after all, being dead. The longer he sat the worse he felt, so there was nothing to be done but get on with it. He jumped down and started pushing his way into the wood, not trying to be quiet particularly, half-hoping he would frighten the girl away and find nothing. He wished he was brave, like boys in books, but the fact was, he wasn't. He was hating every minute of his adventure.

He went further into the wood than he had ever ventured before, until he saw sky ahead, and thought he had come round in a circle and was coming back to the garden again. Lost people were supposed to go round in circles. Thank goodness, he thought, his adventure was nearly over; the girl wasn't there; he could go back and taste the marmalade.

He crashed noisily towards the daylight and was amazed to come out on the edge of a quite big lake. Nobody had ever said there was a lake. Walled gardens, swimming pool and orchard, but no lake. Ben stood looking at it, liking it very much. It was big enough to have a boat on, the sort you could fish in, and there were moorhens making startled noises in the reeds. Their cries echoed in the still trees. It was a very private place, surrounded on all sides by trees.

Ben stood looking at it for quite some time. It was, after all, a terrific discovery, girl or no girl. In fact, he forgot about the girl and about being frightened. He couldn't think about anything but the lake. He went to the edge and saw that it went down quite deep, and there were fish in it (very small ones) and tadpoles that were nearly frogs. He walked along the side, looking in all the time, and came to a place where there was a bit of a beach, the bank shelving up gradually. It was gravelly, fine and soft, and there were footprints in it. Small ones.

He looked up and saw the girl watching him. She was standing in the doorway of a sort of old summer-house that overlooked the beach. It was covered in ivy and very dilapidated, but gave the impression of having been rather smart a long time ago.

She stood there as if it was her house, and her lake, scowling at him.

'What do *you* want?' she asked rudely.

'Nothing. I live here.'

'Well, so do I,' she said.

'You can't.'

'I do.'

Although rude, she didn't seem very frightening at close quarters. She was quite ordinary.

'What's your name?' Ben asked.

'Elfrida.'

'What's the L stand for?'

'Nothing, stupid. It's all the name. Elfrida.'

Ben still didn't get it but didn't like to enquire further. He thought her name was Elf Reader.

'I'm Ben.'

Ben was a good sensible name, he thought, although his mother called him Benjamin and his own Uncle Brownjohn called him Jamboreen and sometimes Jamineb. Uncle Brownjohn was very joky.

'I thought your name was Skylark. What are you poking round here for?'

'You poke round my garden. I've seen you. Coming for water.'

'Oh.' She seemed surprised, and thawed a little in her manner. 'You mustn't tell anyone you've seen me,' she said earnestly. 'You haven't, have you?'

'No. I haven't told Mitzi, that's all there is.'

'Is that your mother? The woman with yellow hair and green shoes?'

'No!' Ben was shocked. 'Mitzi's the Help.'

'What d'you want help for?'

'She looks after me.'

'Why doesn't your mother look after you?'

'She's away. She has to go away. She's an actress.'

'A film star, you mean?'

Ben didn't answer. He didn't like having a film star for a mother. He'd rather have an ordinary one, that stayed at home.

'And your father? Where's he?'

This girl was very nosey. Ben had two fathers, an old one and a new one, but didn't want to tell her this. He went on the attack.

'Where's yours, anyway? Your mother? Does she live here too?'

'No. I live here on my own. Do you want to see my house?'

16

'All right.'

She now seemed quite friendly and talkative. It was hard to tell how old she was, because although she looked quite young, she had a very old and experienced manner, like an adult. Ben guessed at fifteen, but didn't like to ask. He wasn't very good at ages. He had thought Mitzi was forty, but Mitzi said she was twenty-two.

The summer-house had a glass front and double doors but the inside was all lined in dark stained wood and the ceiling was high and pointed. It smelled of dust and decay and old mice, but there was nice furniture in it—a bamboo table and funny old deckchairs with arms and faded seats of flowered chintz. Pushed out of the way at the back was a jumble of old oars, cushions, tennis rackets, croquet sticks, fishing nets, gardening tools, a scythe and an up-ended canoe. The outside was all overgrown with ivy, but Elf had dragged some of it back to let the light in. There were swallows' nests along one of the roof rafters which trailed feathers and horsehair. A black cat was asleep on one of the chairs.

'You cook bacon,' Ben said, remembering. He couldn't see a cooker, only a cardboard box with half a loaf of bread in it, and a few other items.

'I cook outside, on a fire,' Elf said, rather proudly.

Outside, on the edge of the beach, there were two large stones, blackened with fire, and some burnt sticks between. By the edge of the water lay a frying pan and a saucepan, both black on the outside but glittery clean inside.

'I clean them with gravel,' said Elf. 'I wash up with gravel for scouring and moss for wiping. My father taught me.'

Ben was very impressed. Elf was obviously liking to show off her cleverness. Ben was pretty sure that neither of his fathers had any idea how to wash up, either indoors or out, but he thought Uncle Brownjohn might know a thing or two about that sort of thing. It appealed to him, knowing things like that, better than spelling and French.

'What do you cook? Do you go shopping?'

He had never seen her shopping, or going to the shops.

'I cook eggs mostly. I've got hens. Look.'

She took him round the side of the summer-house and showed him a pen of tall wire netting with two brown hens in it. A large, rusty grass-clippings box off a lawn-mower, up-ended and filled with moss, was their egg-laying box. In it was one brown egg, quite large. The hens were scratching contentedly. They were exactly the same as George's hens, which he kept in his back garden.

'When it's dark, I bring them in the house with

me, so the fox won't get them. They perch on the top of the canoe.'

'What do you feed them on?' Ben asked.

'Oh, I find things,' Elf said airily.

They certainly looked very well fed and contented.

'Would you like some tea?' Elf was pleased with Ben's obvious admiration of her efforts, and anxious to demonstrate her talents. Her scowly look had changed to one of eager friendliness, making her look a lot younger and nicer. Ben felt better about this. He agreed to the tea with a sense of warm excitement. His brave adventure was turning out much better than he had suspected it would.

Elf filled the saucepan from the bucket of spring water she had taken from his garden. The bucket looked like one of theirs, which Mitzi had lost a few weeks ago.

In the summer-house she had a pile of dry sticks and moss and straw for tinder.

'It's easy to make a fire if you have dry stuff to start with,' she said, demonstrating. 'Go and fetch some more wood while I get it started.'

She had matches, and a tin plate to put over the saucepan for a lid.

Ben went off to collect wood, smashing around in the trees and dragging out quite big stuff. He was really excited now, making a fire. This was tons better than making marmalade.

'Hey, it's only a cup of tea. Not a four-course meal,' Elf said.

The smoke was curling up, no doubt to drift back through the trees and scent the garden, giving away Elf Reader's existence. Ben was entranced by what was happening, finding this fantastic place.

'I've got chocolate biscuits, if you like.'

While the pan was warming they went back into the summer-house. There was a very old chest of

drawers against one wall, and Elf opened one of the drawers and took out some very elegant, brand-new-looking mugs and teaspoons, and out of another drawer she took teabags and chocolate biscuits and sugar.

'No milk,' she said. 'Milk's difficult. I've got condensed though.'

She opened another drawer in which there were rows of tins, mostly of sausages, baked beans, peaches and cream. Ben was very impressed.

'Where did you get all them from?'

'Mind your own business,' Elf said, quite sharply.

She had a shiny tin-opener with which she opened the tin of condensed milk. She offered it to Ben with a teaspoon.

'Want some?'

They went back to the fire and watched the flames curling round the black saucepan. Ben ate the condensed milk. He felt gorgeously, fantastic-ally happy. The moorhens made their chucking noises out on the lake, the hens scratted and clucked and the black cat came out of the summer-house and rubbed itself round Ben's legs.

'The cat was wild. I tamed it,' Elf said.

She could do anything, Ben thought.

The tin lid rattled on the pan and she deftly flicked it off with a stick and dropped in two teabags. She took the saucepan off the fire and set it on one of the stones.

'Spoon some milk into the mugs,' she ordered.

While the tea brewed she went into the summer-house and came out with two deckchairs, one each, which she set out on the sandy beach.

'There.' She looked at Ben and laughed.

They sat in the deckchairs with their mugs of creamy tea, looking out over the lake.

'Do you live here at night?' Ben asked, wanting to get it right.

'Yes. I live here all the time.'

Ben did not really understand. How could she? he kept thinking.

'Where are your mother and father?' he asked.

'Where are yours then?'

'They're away.'

'Well, I'm away,' Elf said.

There didn't seem to be any answer to that.

They finished the mugs of tea, and Ben washed them up in the lake with gravel, for the condensed milk stuck on the bottom, and some grass. After-wards the mugs were clean but his hands were rather sticky. He wiped them across the front of Skylark. He then thought he had been away rather a long time, enough for Mitzi to have finished the marmalade, and the awful thought that she might

22

come looking for him made him, very reluctantly, decide to go home.

'Will you come again?' Elf asked, as if she wanted him to.

'Yes.'

'You mustn't bring anyone else. You mustn't tell anyone. You mustn't tell that woman where you've been. I'll kill you if anyone finds out about me.'

She stood before him, very fierce and old-looking again, and rather frightening.

'No, I won't. I promise.'

'That's all right then.'

Ben turned and walked back the way he had come, along the lake a bit and then into the wood, he hoped in the direction of the house. Just as he struck off into the trees, Elf called out to him.

'Skylark!'

He turned and waited.

'What?'

She was standing there by her fireplace, watching him.

'Goodbye.'

That was all, as if she had been going to say something, and changed her mind.

Ben walked back in a dream, not getting lost at all. He was so excited by what he had discovered that he knew it would show. He did not know how to go into the kitchen as if nothing had happened, when it had. He couldn't act, like his mother.

Luckily for him George was there, because one of the bullocks was a bit seedy-like, he said, so Ben went with George and looked down the animal's throat and gave it a drench, which was a pretty mucky business, and by the time he went in, his great flush of excitement had cooled to a more manageable hop-and-skippy feeling which he could have got from some other things.

As it was, when Mitzi questioned him sharply— 'Wherever have you been? I was getting quite worried,'—he could answer quite honestly, 'I was helping George. I was only outside.'

'Look at my marmalade then. What do you think of that?'

She obviously thought a lot of it herself, from the way she stood admiring the rows of orange jars, her yellow frizz hair stuck down on her forehead, orange pips peppering the front of her purple jumper.

'It looks very nice,' he said politely. Not nearly as good as the mug of tea with condensed milk, he thought, but didn't say.

'Yeah, good isn't it?'

Ben took off Skylark and they had toast and hot marmalade for tea, because they wanted to try it. It was rather runny, and ran off the toast, and they both got very sticky.

'It's good though,' Mitzi kept saying.

She really wasn't any good at anything, Ben thought sadly. He was sorry for her. Not like Elf, who could do absolutely everything.

'We're going up to London next week. You've got a reminder from the dentist, for next Wednesday.'

'I don't want to go to London.'

'Bad luck,' said Mitzi. 'Because I do. Besides, you've got to. Your ma expects me to do things like that. Take you to the dentist, I mean.'

'Why London?'

He knew there was a dentist in the town nearby, because he had read the brass plate and seen him through the window.

'Your ma, being so smart, goes to Harley Street for things like that. It's just the way she is. You've got to lump it.'

Harley Street, Ben remembered, was a very boring street of tall houses, all of which bore brass plates to say a doctor or a dentist worked there.

'There's nothing wrong with my teeth,' he said. Even the condensed milk hadn't made them jump.

'Good. We'll be in and out then.'

If he hadn't met Elf, he would have been quite

keen to go—not to the dentist, but the getting there and back was fun and Mitzi tended to buy him ice cream and chips and things when they went out. But, having met Elf, he could think of nothing but going to visit her again.

When it was dark that night, and he was lying in bed thinking about the marvellous thing that had happened to him, he heard the rain start to patter on the roof and the wind whirl about in the trees on the lawn. He got out of bed and went to the window and looked out. It was very dark, with just a few stars whisking in and out of the black clouds. The dead trees were scratching together and the thick branch of the wistaria knocked on the window below like a ghost trying to get in.

He thought of Elf down there by the lake, lying on a deckchair in her summer-house with the hens perched on the canoe, listening to the storm in the trees and the lapping of the agitated lake against her private beach, all alone. Splendidly, frighteningly alone. Was she frightened? Ben felt all strung up, pretending to be Elf. The old house was solid around him like a rock and Mitzi was just across the passage reading *Seventeen* magazine in bed (although she was twenty-two)—he could see the strip of light under her door if he went to his own and looked out. But Elf had no Mitzi. Elf had nobody.

3

Oscar
A brave dog
1929~
1938

The next morning Ben was away to the wood as soon as he had had breakfast, declining Mitzi's offer to take him shopping with her. Mitzi was surprised but, he could see, quite pleased, as it meant she could linger in the dress shops and read over her coffee in The Copper Kettle. She checked the strings on Skylark severely, and said, 'Don't you get into any mischief now.'

'Oh no,' said Ben.

When he got to the summer-house, he felt Elf was waiting for him, although she made her 'Hallo' sound very casual.

'Can you stay to dinner?' she asked. 'I could

make something special.'

'If I'm not back Mitzi'll start looking for me.'

'We could have it early.'

'Oh, yes!' Ben did not want to miss a special dinner.

'We could have it now, if you like.'

Elf was full of good ideas. 'Yes. Let's. Shall I collect some wood?'

'Yes. And I'll light the fire.'

They worked together like old hands. Ben felt the lovely, unfamiliar warmth of friendship overtake him—Elf accepted him and talked to him like an equal, and he strove to do everything just as she liked it, as he wanted so badly to keep her goodwill. She did not treat him like a little boy. She treated him like someone old and clever.

For dinner she made a line of tins on the beach: sausages, baked beans, new potatoes, carrots and asparagus tips. For pudding there were pears, tangerines, custard and rice pudding, also in tins.

'We'll put it all in together,' she said. 'Not the pudding.'

She laughed. The shiny tin-opener whizzed round the tins. Mitzi always got stuck with tin-openers, and swore a lot and cut her finger, but Elf swept off the lids in a moment. Ben emptied them with splodgy, sucking noises into the big billycan. They stirred the ingredients round with a large spoon and set it over the flames. It looked a lot for two, Ben thought.

'You could stay the night, if you like,' Elf said.

Ben considered. He did not see how he could.

'You get out, after that Mitzi's gone to bed,' Elf suggested.

The thought of it made Ben prickle with excitement. Or fear, he wasn't sure which. The thought of climbing the wall in the dark and going into the wood wasn't too good, but the thought of sleeping with Elf in the summer-house was fantastic. He would need Oscar for the first bit.

'I could come and meet you,' Elf said, as if she knew.

'I could signal, when Mitzi goes to bed! Flash the light on and off!' He liked that idea enormously.

'I could wait on the wall, until you signalled.'

'But in the morning . . . ?'

'We'd wake up early, and you could go back before that Mitzi wakes up. She'd never know.'

'How would we know the time?'

'Oh, you can tell. We can use an alarm clock.'

'You haven't got an alarm clock.'

'No. But I will have. I can get one. Or a nice watch. It would be nice to have a watch.'

Ben couldn't think of any more objections. He was so excited he felt quite sick.

'When can I come?'

'Tomorrow night. Say tomorrow night.'

The dinner was starting to bubble. Elf fetched some plates and after another good stir, spooned the mixture out into two equal portions. They were enormous. She sent Ben for knives and forks, and they sat down to eat. It was too much for Ben, but he ate it all, knowing Elf would not like him to leave any. Then there was the pudding. By the end of pudding Ben felt afraid to move in case he burst. He was proud of his capacity, proud of not letting Elf down.

'I bet I'm a better cook than that Mitzi,' Elf said.

'Yes, you are. Her marmalade's not much good.'

He felt a bit remorseful as soon as he had said that, remembering how pleased she had been. Perhaps marmalade was difficult. He didn't know.

'Are you always going to live here?' he asked.

'No, of course not. I'm waiting for my father to come home.'

'Home from where?'

'From sea. He's in the merchant navy.'

'When's he coming then?'

'In June some time.'

'Does he know you're here?'

'No, of course he doesn't. Nobody knows. Only you.' She fixed him with her fierce glare. 'And you're not telling anyone, are you?'

'No!'

They washed up and gave the hens a left-over potato, and the cat half a sausage Elf had kept for him, then Ben thought he had better go to get home before Mitzi arrived back from shopping.

'And tomorrow night, you'll come, won't you?' Elf asked, fierce again.

'Yes. Yes, I will!'

'I'll wait for you on the wall.'

'I'll come, I promise!'

Just to say it made his heart bump fearsomely. But it was a delicious kind of fear, for something he wanted to do terribly.

'Okay, Skylark, I believe you.' Elf smiled.

'Goodbye then.'

'Goodbye, Skylark.'

Ben made off for the house, full to bursting. Physically it was with dinner, but his mind felt as full as his stomach, stretched with amazing things to think about.

When he got back, Mitzi was just getting out of the Mini. She had a large, steaming plastic bag.

'Look, I got fish and chips—your favourite! I knew you'd be pleased. Big portions too! Hurry up, let's have it while it's still hot!'

She rushed into the kitchen and got out the plates and the ketchup while Ben felt the sausages and the baked beans and the asparagus tips and the pears and the custard all clamouring inside him, asking

31

not to be joined by fish and chips. There's no room down here, they were all saying, very loudly, very decided. He sat wanly down at the table.

'I don't feel well.'

'You're hungry. This'll put you right.'

Mitzi emptied the paperful out on his plate, and the fish and chips steamed up into his face. He had to get up and go, and Mitzi made him lie down and gave him milk of magnesia. She ate his fish and chips as well as her own, and afterwards she lay down too, and started on her new *Seventeen*.

'You'd better not be ill,' she said. 'We're going to London on Wednesday, remember. We don't want to miss that, do we?'

Wednesday was the day he had to get home from Elf's summer-house and in bed in time to wake up. He couldn't stop thinking about it. He thought about it solidly for the rest of that day, and all the next day, until it was just about time to go. He lay in bed waiting to hear Mitzi come upstairs and shut her bedroom door. He was shivering all over, although he wasn't cold. He had to take a blanket, Elf had said, because she only had one sleeping-bag. But there were lots of cushions. She would make his bed up all ready.

Mitzi was reading in bed. It seemed like hours before at last her light went out. Even then Ben waited, so that she would go to sleep. Then he got up and dressed and switched his light on and off twice, for the signal. Suppose Elf wasn't there? Ben felt clumsy with excitement. Every little move creaked and sighed through the old house; he could not believe he was having this great adventure. Suppose Mitzi heard him? He was fully dressed and had his blanket rolled up under his arm. Perhaps he could pretend he was sleep-walking. People did, he knew.

He opened his door and tiptoed out. The stairs creaked dreadfully. He had never noticed how much in the daylight. Eergh, argh, aaargh, eee-eergh . . . steadily down, and no sound from Mitzi's room. Down to the flagstones, blessedly silent and solid. He padded along to the outside door and quietly pulled back the bolts which Uncle Brown-john had oiled on his last visit. At last, he was outside, the cold night air striking his bed-warm body so that he shivered. He stood on the steps a moment, smelling the stars, his blood racing.

At the bottom of the walled garden, two flashes of light blinked at him. Elf really was waiting! The relief stopped his shivers instantly and he almost shouted out with joy. He ran blindly into the darkness, over the old lawn and past Oscar's gravestone.

'Come on, Oscar!' he called out as he passed, and imagined the dog jumping up out of his grave at the

33

sound of running feet. A beam of light sprung out at him from the top of the wall and he heard Elf's voice.

'Up here! I've been waiting simply ages!'

'I saw your signal,' Ben said, scrambling up.

'Yes. I got a watch and a torch. I thought it would be useful. Look.'

She shone the torch on her wrist where a bright new digital watch with a red strap glittered back. Ben was very impressed. It said 23.22.

'Nice, isn't it?'

'Did you buy it? Did you go shopping?'

'Yes.'

Ben thought she must be very rich. The torch was a big, important one with a handle, not just a little sticky thing. It beamed the way through the wood and they found the lake without trouble. A candle was flickering in the summer-house, stuck in a lemonade bottle, and Elf switched off the torch and let Ben take in his new bedroom. She had pulled out one of the old deckchairs and set it down very low and put cushions on it. Her rumpled sleeping-bag lay on another. The doors were open to the lake, and now that Ben's eyes were used to the dark he could see the water gleaming. There was no wind and it was quite still save for the strange night noises of the birds and invisible mammals in the grass, which Ben was used to. He lay down on his new bed and Elf arranged the blanket over him.

'There. I've got an alarm clock too. I've set it for six o'clock. That Mitzi doesn't get up very early, does she?'

'We're going to London tomorrow.'

'Not at six o'clock?'

'No.'

'Six o'clock'll do then.'

Perhaps Elf thought Ben would sleep as soundly as herself, but Ben lay awake just about all night, staring out at the lake. It was as good as sleeping outside altogether. The air smelled definitely of outside, damp and rich and earthy, nothing in it of old dust and long-ago polish that characterized the house at the top of the garden. The same owl he heard from his bedroom was much closer now, and in the first faint light of dawn a ghostly heron flew down and stood motionless on the beach where they had their fire, silhouetted against the water. Ben lay watching, hardly daring to breathe, but the heron, at home, was unaware. Fine streamers of mist hung above the water, blurring the distance. It was far too exciting to sleep, and when the hens, perched on the canoe, decided that day had started and jumped down with a rattle of wings, Ben sat up and looked at Elf's alarm clock. It said, he thought (he was not too good at telling the time) half past four. The hens scratted past him and went outside and the heron flew away.

Elf lay on her back, her arm with the shiny new watch flung out above her head. Ben got up and looked at her watch. Yes. It said 04.32.

'Your hens are loose,' he said anxiously. 'They've gone out.'

She opened her eyes and saw him, smiled. Yawned.

'They don't go away,' she said. 'It's all right.'

She sat up and looked at the clock.

'Hey, it's miles too early!'

'Too early for what?'

Elf remembered her new watch and looked at it proudly. 'It's nice, isn't it? I'm really glad I got this watch.'

'Can we get up?'

'You look up to me.'

'Are you getting up?'

Elf wriggled out of her sleeping-bag and stood up.

'There. I'm up.'

It was gloriously simple and quick, not like home. Only shoes to do and they were ready.

'You needn't go home yet, need you?' Elf said. 'That Mitzi'll be snoring for ages yet.'

'No.'

Now he was actually up it felt very cold, and he shivered.

Elf noticed and said, 'We'll light a fire.'

Ben loved lighting fires. He got the dry sticks out, and Elf soon had the flames licking up her little wigwam of twigs. Ben went to get more wood, but the grass and the undergrowth were soaked with dew, and icy.

'Don't bother. There's enough here.'

Elf, the good housewife, had a store inside. 'It's always like this in the morning. I collect it in the day, when it's dried off.'

They sat close to the flames, holding out their hands to the warmth, and sometimes turning round so that their bottoms got warm. The hens came down to the water's edge and had a drink, and the streamers of mist slipped away as the first faint sun started to slant through the trees. A thrush sang deep in the wood, a daylight bird to take the place of the owl and the secretive heron.

Elf kept looking at her watch admiringly.

'You ought to go,' she said.

38

'Oh no!'

The time had flown.

'I wish I could live here with you!'

'You can't, Skylark.'

'I'm not Skylark.'

'You are usually.'

He hadn't stopped to put the life-jacket on last night. He felt gloriously free as he walked back through the wood. Elf came with him to get some drinking water from the spring. They climbed the wall and dropped down into the garden. Ben thought of Oscar jumping back into the quiet of his grave, and picked some dandelions, and put them in the jam jar. He brought the jam jar to the spring and filled it, and put it back on the grave.

'You are funny,' Elf said.

Ben didn't think so.

Today he had got to go to London, he thought. He felt rather tired. He watched Elf depart with her bucket of water, and let himself quietly into the house, remembering to put back the bolts which he had had to leave undone. He went upstairs and undressed and put his pyjamas on and got into bed and fell deeply asleep.

4

The next thing Ben knew was Mitzi shaking him and saying, 'Whatever's wrong with you?'

She looked alarmed.

'I thought you were never going to wake up! Come on, we're going to London. I thought you'd be up extra early.'

She had her best clothes on, which Ben thought were very peculiar. She wore a very tight purple skirt which held her knees together so she could hardly walk and then flared out when it was too late. On top she had a yellow blouse with black spots on and a bright pink sort of sloppy jacket, and a lot of gold chains round her neck and about ten jangly bracelets on each wrist. Her shoes were gold and spiky, with a lot of straps.

She pulled his blankets back, then wrinkled her nose and sniffed.

'What's that smell? Like smoke?'

Ben couldn't smell anything.

Mitzi bent down towards him and sniffed again.

'You smell all smoky!'

Ben kept quiet.

'You're all dirty! Didn't you wash properly last night?'

Just about to deny indignantly that he hadn't washed, Ben quickly thought to say no, he hadn't, to account for the dirt. Mitzi had been watching a play on television about ants that grew to the size of Alsatian dogs and hadn't been able to tear herself away to supervise his washing.

Mitzi said all the proper things about his being old enough to wash himself without her supervising him, and what would his mother think of him, then went down to get breakfast. Ben got up and found his shoes were all muddy. Wet muddy. Lucky she hadn't noticed them. He cleaned them in the wash-bowl in the bathroom with the lavatory brush, but got rather a lot of mud all over the place. It sprang up from the brush in a sort of spray all over everything. By the time he had wiped it all up with

41

the bath-towel Mitzi was shouting at him, what on earth was he doing?

He did feel very tired.

Mitzi drove the Mini halfway to London and parked it in the car park of a station which was on a tube line. Ben liked the tube train as a rule but today kept nodding off as he looked out of the window. Mitzi was engrossed in a novel called *Her Heart in Exchange* and did not notice until he fell off the seat at Bethnal Green.

'Whatever's the matter with you?' she asked crossly.

'I slipped.'

She gave him a hard look, and put her book away, and he managed to keep awake until they got off at Oxford Circus. Ben had already learned that there was no circus at Oxford Circus, only an awful lot of people and traffic all trying to go in different directions, so there was no disappointment this time. They went to the dentist and his teeth were all right, so then Mitzi trailed him round a few shops, and took him to Hamleys the toyshop, and kept him well fed with ice cream and hamburgers and chips, and he still managed to keep awake until they got back to Liverpool Street Station. It was here that he saw something that kept him wide awake for the rest of the day—forever, he thought.

Mitzi had gone to the loo and he was standing still as instructed against a wall, waiting for her. On the wall were a few posters about Saver tickets, and going to see your old granny cheap, and one about watching out for pickpockets. At the end of the row was one headed:

MISSING PERSON

Underneath was a photo of a scowling girl and underneath that it said: 'Have you seen Elfrida Cvitanovich, missing from home since April 2nd? She is 14 years old, with black curly hair and brown eyes, 5 ft 4 ins (1.63 m) tall, of medium build, and wearing jeans, a blue T–shirt, navy jersey and a grey anorak.'

Underneath that, in larger letters, it said: '£1,000 reward is offered to anyone with information as to her whereabouts.'

'Oh, look at that—my thousand pounds!'

So engrossed was Ben in reading—with difficulty—the momentous poster that he had not noticed Mitzi's return. She stood beside him, curious as to what had fixed his attention.

'Fancy, Ben—if we found her! Set me up for life that would! Pigs might fly, eh?'

She gave a great, sad sigh. Pigs might fly was one of the things she said quite often.

'Would you tell them?' Ben asked.

'Tell them I'd found her? You bet I would!'

'She might not want to be found!'

'So? She's no right to go missing at that age. It would be doing her a service, turning her in.'

Ben, deeply disturbed by finding Elf in the poster, was even more disturbed by what Mitzi said. What if Mitzi knew!—why he was sleepy, why he smelled smoky, where he disappeared to—Mitzi only had to look out at the right moment, and she would see her thousand pounds filling a bucket at the spring pool. He would have to warn Elf! Did she know there were posters up about her, offering a thousand pounds? She must be terribly valuable, he thought, to have a thousand pounds offered for her. He wondered if his parents would offer a thousand pounds for him if he ran off? If they would, he could run off for a bit and then let Mitzi know where he was, and she could tell them and collect the thousand pounds that way ... His mind was racing as he trailed after Mitzi down the busy platform. But he had nowhere to run to, only to Elf in the summer-house, and on no account did he want Elf to get found too.

He fell asleep in the train going home, but Mitzi did not worry about it this time. When they got home there was no chance of seeing Elf and although he intended to go out to her after Mitzi was asleep, he never remembered anything else until he was awoken by tapping on his window. Opening his eyes in alarm, he saw that it was already light. The whole night had passed. He remembered that he had had to do something important but couldn't remember what, until the pattering sound came on his window again. He got out of bed and looked out and saw Elf standing on the kitchen steps below, getting ready to throw more gravel at his window. Then the memory of the poster came back in a great rush and he very nearly screamed out at her, to tell her to go away. What was she doing, standing on his doorstep? Mitzi only had to wake up . . .

He ran downstairs, almost falling down them in his hurry, and went to the kitchen door. He slid the bolts back and opened it.

'Hallo, Skylark! It's your turn to have me to breakfast! Let me in! That Mitzi won't be waking up for ages yet, will she? Look, I've brought you a present!'

And she held up a glittery digital watch, just the same as her own but with a bright yellow strap.

'It's for you, Skylark. Aren't you pleased?'

Ben's brain whirled. He was in a great muddle.

'Elf, you mustn't!' He didn't know what to say. Mustn't what? She was already indoors, sitting on the kitchen table.

'Yesterday, in London, I saw . . .'

Elf was jumping off now and filling the kettle.

'The Queen?' She laughed. 'What's the matter with you? Aren't you pleased to see me?'

'I saw . . .'

'Don't you like the watch? Honestly, it's for you.'

'It's lovely . . .'

'Hold out your arm.'

She snatched it up and buckled the watch round his wrist.

'There! Just like mine.'

She held out her red one beside his. They both said 06.34.

'You mustn't come here,' Ben blurted out. 'You mustn't!'

'That's not very nice,' Elf said. 'After I've brought you a present like that.'

'There's a poster with your photo on it. In London.'

'What do you mean?'

'It says "Thousand Pounds Reward". For you! I saw it—yesterday. I was going to come and tell you.'

'You're joking!'

'No, I'm not. I saw it, I tell you! Mitzi saw it too.'

'Where?'

'On Liverpool Street Station. Everyone can see it. Your photo and your name underneath and

46

it says "Missing Person".'

'I don't believe you!'

'Honestly. It's true.'

'What photo?'

'What do you mean, what photo? It's you—I recognized you. Looking cross. And your name.'

'It's a school photo. Is it a school photo?'

'I don't know!'

'Nobody ever took a photo of me. Only at school. What am I wearing?'

'Just ordinary things. I don't know!' Ben could not see that it mattered.

'You mean, it's up for everyone to see? My photo and my name?'

'Yes. And "missing person—a thousand pounds reward".'

'My ma hasn't got a thousand pounds. That's rubbish.'

'But, Elf—if anyone recognizes you—like Mitzi, she will if she sees you, don't you see . . . '

'I mustn't be found, not till my father comes. They'll take me away, my ma and her boyfriend. They don't want my father to have me, they don't want me to go with him. They want me to go with them. But I don't want to. I won't! I won't.'

She spoke very loudly and had gone all red and excited. Ben had never seen her look like that before. Her eyes glittered and he thought they had tears in them. But he knew Elf would never cry.

'Do be quiet,' he said. 'Or Mitzi will hear you.'

He was really worried, wishing Elf would go away, and feeling bad about not wanting her. But Mitzi would sell Elf in a flash to get her thousand pounds. Elf had no idea how badly Mitzi wanted her thousand pounds.

Dreading to hear sounds from the stairs, Ben suddenly heard sounds from out in the yard—the wheels of a large car on the gravel. At any time this would have been a surprise, but at 06.37 in the morning it was unheard-of. There was a scrunch of stopping and then door-slamming and voices. Ben leapt to the window.

It was his mother and Uncle Brownjohn, gathering up bags and parcels and laughing. Ben's mouth dropped open.

'It's my mother!'

He turned round and saw Elf, no longer red and cross, but white and scared.

'What shall I do?' she said.

'They're coming in! Quick!'

He caught her arm and dragged her across to the door into the hall.

'You can go out the front way.'

He opened the door, and as he did so Mitzi's

48

voice floated down from the top of the stairs.

'Ben! Ben, are you up?'

The top stair groaned as Mitzi's weight came on it.

There was no time for Elf to reach the front door. No time to reach the doors that led into the sitting-room on one side of the hall and the dining-room on the other, without Mitzi seeing her. The only possibility was the door into the big old-fashioned pantry. Ben pushed it open and Elf darted in just as Ben's mother and Uncle Brownjohn came into the kitchen from the yard. Ben turned round, and his mother saw him standing in the doorway in his pyjamas as if he had just come downstairs.

'Darling! Darling Benjamin! Look who's here! Isn't this a lovely surprise? Come and give me a kiss!'

Although he did not move, he was swept up immediately in a great furry hug, engulfed in exotic smells, scraped and pricked by spiky earrings and knuckleduster rings. His mother was always like this, even at 06.38 in the morning. He could not think of anything to say at all.

'Aren't you pleased to see me? And your Uncle John? He met me at the airport and is going to stay for a few days. Isn't that lovely? Give him a kiss! Darling Benjamin!'

She hugged and kissed him six times more, nearly

knocking him out, then turned to greet Mitzi who
was standing in the doorway looking stunned.

'Why, Mrs Harkaway, you never said you were
coming!'

'Dear Mitzi, such a surprise! I never knew myself,
darling! There's a three-week hold-up in the

schedule—some tedious budget argument—and I'm not wanted until the first of June, so I just got on a plane and here I am! There was no time to let you know! Oh, isn't it lovely to be home! Isn't this a lovely place, John darling? Do put the kettle on, Mitzi dear, and we can all have breakfast.'

Ben said, 'Mitzi made some marmalade. Shall I fetch it?'

If anyone was going to fetch marmalade it was going to be him, because of Elf. However was she going to get out?

His mother always made such a racket and fuss, leaving a trail of discarded bits and pieces behind her—fur coat flung over a chair, handbag spilling purses and make-up on the doormat, suitcase on the table, umbrella on the Aga stove . . . but Uncle Brownjohn stood like a great rock, smiling gently, not moving. Ben looked at him and smiled back, feeling that with Uncle Brownjohn on the scene some of his worries might get worked out. He couldn't possibly see how, but the presence was reassuring.

'How's Jamineb then?' his uncle asked. 'What's he up to, so early?'

As if he knew. A very piercing bright blue stare, but kindly.

'Jamboreen the Tambourine,' he said. That was another name he used. 'Are you happy?'

51

'Usually,' Ben said. Not just at that moment though.

'Oh, what a lovely watch your mummy's brought you!' Mitzi said to him. 'Aren't you a lucky boy!'

She was taking the teapot to the back door to empty the tea-leaves out in the flower-bed, as she always did. Ben mumbled something and was aware of his uncle's bright blue stare, quizzical. He followed Mitzi to the back door, suddenly shy. Mitzi, after all, was the one he was at home with. Mitzi opened the door and said, 'Why, there's my bucket that I lost! Wherever's that sprung from?'

Elf's water bucket was standing by the spring pool across the yard.

'Fancy that,' Mitzi said.

She emptied the teapot and took it back to the kitchen.

'I'll get the marmalade,' Ben said hastily. 'I'll get the things out of the pantry.'

'You ought to get dressed, darling!' his mother trilled, gathering up some of her possessions and dropping a few more as she did so. 'I'll just go and put something comfortable on, then we'll all have breakfast together.'

That meant when it was ready, when *they* had made it. Uncle Brownjohn started to lay the table and Ben rushed out to the pantry before Mitzi went. Elf was standing against the far wall, underneath the window, looking petrified. The window was barred.

'I can't get out! What shall I do?' she whispered.

If she had looked brave and in command as she usually did, Ben would have been reassured, but she looked more frightened than he felt already. She certainly couldn't stay there. Ben took a quick glance all round and decided that to act fast was the only solution.

'Quickly—come on!'

His mother was halfway up the stairs and disappearing; Mitzi and his uncle were in the kitchen with their backs to them. Ben stood to one side to let Elf through and she bolted—but silently—like a rabbit, out of the door and into the hall. Ben sprang after her, grabbed her by the arm and deflected her into the sitting-room. The front door was always hard to open, as it was never used, and the best chance of Elf getting out was through the sitting-room window, which Ben knew opened easily.

'Here!'

He slid up the sash and Elf was over the sill in a flash, dropping down into the spiky embrace of the roses that grew rampant in a once well-tended rose-bed. Ben slid the window back instantly and had a last anguished glance from Elf looking back at him. Her face was all horror and despair, not at all her normal look of confidence and scorn, but Ben had to leave her to it. There was no other way. As it was, when he got out into the hall again Uncle Brownjohn was there, looking for him.

'Thought you were getting the marmalade?' he said. He had an easy and kindly way of speaking, but eyes that seemed to know exactly what you were up to. They went past Ben to the window and what they saw Ben could not tell, for he now had his back to it, but their expression did not change. With luck, Elf was still out of sight in the prickly roses.

'I—I just . . . ' He couldn't think of anything very convincing. 'I thought Mitzi left the marmalade in here.'

'How very odd,' said Uncle Brownjohn.

He put his hand on Ben's shoulder and steered him towards the stairs. 'Go and get dressed. I'll get the breakfast.'

5

Ben was in a great muddle of anxiety and excitement and terrified of saying the wrong thing, and over breakfast he had to struggle not to give away any secrets when his mother kept questioning him about what he had been up to.

'He plays beautifully by himself. He's never any trouble,' Mitzi said loyally.

'He doesn't take after me then. I hate being alone,' said Ben's mother. 'In fact, I must ring up Peter and tell him I'm back, and perhaps Alex would like to come over—and Marty too! You'd like that, Benjamin darling, wouldn't you?'

Ben nodded glumly. Peter was his new father and Alex his old—or the other way round, he couldn't remember. He had seen very little of either of them and liked his own Uncle Brownjohn far better than both.

'It's just as well Ben doesn't mind being alone,' Uncle Brownjohn said rather sternly to Ben's mother.

'Whatever do you mean, dear?'

'Such a strange life for a child!'

'He's got everything he wants, surely?'

'Has he?' said Uncle Brownjohn.

Ben began to wonder about what he hadn't got, hoping no one would ask. Fortunately they didn't. He never understood what his mother was talking about half the time, and supposed it was because he wasn't used to her. He understood Mitzi. She was quite easy.

He understood Mitzi being amazed when she went to fetch her lost bucket, and found it had gone again. Elf had filled it and taken it back with her.

'Am I seeing things?' she asked Ben. 'It was there, wasn't it?'

Ben shrugged, not wanting to take sides.

'I swear it was. I saw it. Oh dear.' She was upset, with Ben's mother arriving and inviting all her friends and relations. She was going to have to cook, she feared. It was not what she was employed for; she was employed for looking after and teaching Ben, and now she knew she hadn't done that very well either, if anyone started asking. When Ben went out he put Skylark on as a matter of course, and now his mother and Uncle Brownjohn were staring at his strange figure in the doorway, engulfed in the large, faded life-jacket.

'What on earth is that for? Where's the boat?'

'What boat?' said Ben.

'Skylark.'

Ben didn't know what to say.

'Take it off, darling. You're not at sea,' his mother said.

Ben felt as if he was.

'Mitzi said . . . ' He stopped.

'Oh dear. Mitzi,' said his mother.

Now, as well as worrying about Elf, Ben had Mitzi to worry about. Suppose his mother gave Mitzi the sack? She was always going on about a roof over her head. He imagined Mitzi living in the summer-house with Elf and cooking her breakfast over the fire by the lakeside.

'Mitzi's good,' he said loyally. 'I like her.'

'That's what matters,' said Uncle Brownjohn.

His mother looked cross.

'I don't think your mother knows what children require,' Uncle Brownjohn said to Ben.

'What do children require?' asked Ben politely.

'More than you've got, Jamboreen the Tambourine.'

His mother went to the phone and rang all her relations and quite soon they arrived, with an enormous amount of embracing and exclaiming and general noise. Ben had to be kissed a lot and told many times over how he'd grown. It was terrible. He called the wrong one 'Daddy', and caused a moment of stunned embarrassment. How could he tell? The last time he had seen him—and that was two years ago—he had had a beard and hardly any hair, and this time he was clean-shaven and had hair down to his collar. Ben buried his face in Uncle Brownjohn's comfortable jersied stomach and felt a comforting arm encircle him.

Uncle Brownjohn said to him, 'Don't worry, Jamboreen, they don't know who they are themselves very often. They are actors and play parts all the time.'

Ben didn't understand. 'Are you an actor?'

'No. I'm a writer. It's quite different. It's much quieter.'

The actors ate and drank all through the evening and talked and laughed very loudly and Ben had to stay up with them.

Outside in the garden it was still and dark. Bats tumbled and squeaked in the outside light over the kitchen door. Ben, escaping for a few minutes, stood looking, sniffing the warm, thunderous air. He wanted desperately to go down the garden to

Elf, even just to Oscar, but they kept calling him and hugging him and wanting him to talk and sit on their knees and eat chocolates.

Ben knew Elf needed him. He'd remembered her last white, anxious look. When at last he went to bed, just before midnight, he meant to wake up early and go down and see her while everyone was still asleep, but he was so tired he never woke up until nine o'clock when all the actors started groaning for cups of coffee and blundering about looking for the bathroom and complaining of the cold.

It was the beginning of another noisy, crowded day. It was Sunday and his mother was going to make a complicated Sunday lunch with roast beef and Yorkshire pudding and roast potatoes and peas and apple pie and cream, and she was making a lot of fuss about it already. Somebody drove off and fetched an armful of Sunday newspapers and the whole house was full of people reading papers and drinking coffee and peeling potatoes and watching television and all talking nineteen to the dozen and wandering about dropping cigarette ash every-where. Ben tried to keep out of the way but they were everywhere, with even more of them arriving for lunch.

Mitzi, her face as red as her shirt and all screwed up with frightful anxiety, was organizing the dinner, which Ben knew was not her thing at all:

she wasn't brilliant even at baked beans or sausages, which were always underdone or overdone or stuck to the pan. But there was little he could do to help her. His head reeling at the awfulness of everything, he took advantage of a lull in the kissing and patting and 'Ben darlings' to escape out of the back door and into the garden.

He walked down as far as Oscar's grave and stood breathing in the quiet and the friendliness of his familiar domain. Then, with a soft call to Oscar to come, he started off for the broken wall, hesitant at first and then, with a sudden longing for the sweet sense of Elf's summer-house life, faster, hurrying, stumbling in his eagerness. Over the wall and, with Oscar's ghost bounding ahead, crashing through the brambles and branches to the silent lipping of the lake water on the soft beach, the smell of wood-smoke on the misty-blue-grey morning, and the welcome sight of Elf's four-square figure putting fresh branches on her fire.

She was looking up with great alarm, half poised for flight, until she saw who it was, when her face crumpled with relief.

'Oh, Skylark, you've come!'

Her obvious pleasure was a great pleasure to Ben. The relief he felt to be with her was almost as great as hers.

'What's going on at your place?' she asked.

Ben explained.

'They don't know about me? You haven't told them?'

'No. Of course not.'

'You haven't told that Mitzi?'

'No.'

Reassured, Elf got out the deckchairs and the cushions and they sat side by side on the beach. Far away over the water meadows they could hear the church bell bonging away from the town, soothing and hypnotic. Ben felt that everything was all right again, his world in order. The hens clucked busily and the wild cat slept on the summer-house roof in the sun. Then he remembered that Elf was worth a thousand pounds and people were looking for her. She wasn't just someone camping in his garden, but a Missing Person with her face pasted up on walls all over London. He looked at her sideways, to see if she looked any different now that he knew she was different, and noticed that yes, she looked thinner somehow, and older, and crosser. He didn't like to say anything to spoil feeling glad to be back with her, but after a while she said, 'What am I going to do, Skylark?'

Ben felt like saying, 'What am I going to do?' There was no answer for either of them.

'Just stay here. I'll stay with you.'

He need never go back, he thought. At least, not

till they'd all gone. They'd never miss him, all that noise and business.

'I can't go out now,' Elf said.

'You are out.'

'I mean shopping. In case I'm caught.'

'You don't need to,' Ben said, remembering all the rows of tins in her chest of drawers. 'You've got enough.'

Elf wriggled in her deckchair.

'I like going shopping.'

Ben remembered the yellow watch on his wrist, and the big torch, and the shiny tin-opener, all of the best, and wondered again how she was so rich. Hens, too, cost at least five pounds each.

'Have you got a lot of money?'

'No. I haven't any.'

She must have spent it all. 'You can't go shopping then, can you?'

Elf didn't answer.

Ben remembered that she was waiting for her father to come home from the merchant navy.

'How will your father find you here?'

'He won't. I shall have to find him. That's the trouble.'

And to Ben's dismay she started to cry. He didn't like to look, and carefully watched the lake instead, but his heart was thumping with misery and anxiety. Mitzi was in trouble, too, trying to cook dinner and being found wanting, and Elf, who was clever and brave and scornful and had an answer for everything, was crying.

'I'll find him for you,' he said desperately.

'How can you?' A touch of scorn nettled her choky voice and Ben felt slightly better. But didn't know how he could find her father. He could not even pronounce her father's name.

Elf gave a great sniff and stopped crying as suddenly as she had started.

'What shall we have for dinner?'

This was better.

'I'll collect some wood,' he said, scrambling out of the deckchair.

There was further to go these days, all the big bits nearby having been used up. But Ben was beginning to know the wood fairly well—it was not nearly as big as he had first supposed, and he would never get lost in it now. It was a friendly, comforting place, bounded securely by the garden on one side, the lake on the opposite side, a green wheatfield to the south and the water meadows going down to the canal on the north side, not the vast, dark, everlasting forest that he had first imagined.

He revived Elf's breakfast fire with some small twigs and Elf's spirits revived too as they started their domestic tasks. The sun shafted strongly through the trees, bringing the smells of blossom and the soft balsam smell of the poplars on the boundary of the wheatfield, and the thin haze of smoke hung blue in the sunlight like a veil, adding its scent. How much more satisfactory, Ben thought, than the sweat and bad temper he had left round the Aga at home. He really loved cooking over Elf's fire and cleaning the pans in the lake with gravel. It was like real life, not boring ordinary life with Mitzi.

Elf's spirits lifted and she cottoned on to Oscar's ghost and started throwing sticks into the lake for him to fetch while Ben tended the thick concoction she had produced in the big billy. After dinner they set about making the hens a new run on a fresh patch of earth and grass, making a fence of interlaced branches. Luckily the hens were not a very agile breed, too heavy to fly over, or at least not inclined to do so.

'They're full of eggs,' Ben said. 'Like bombs in a bomber.'

'They lay a lot. Always one each a day. Do you want eggs for tea?'

They put a billy on to boil. Ben could smell the smoke in his jersey and wondered if anyone at home would smell him like Mitzi had done. But they all smelled pretty smoky themselves, he remembered, and aftershavy too, very strong. He would be fairly safe this time. He sat timing the eggs carefully with his yellow wrist-watch. Elf said four minutes or even four and a half, because they were big. She was getting out eggcups, and tea-spoons, and salt.

Ben was crouched over the fire, concentrating hard. A large shadow suddenly fell over his watch and a voice said, 'So this is where you get to.'

He looked up in surprise and saw Uncle Brown-john standing above him, smiling. His heart missed several beats, and he could not think of anything to say.

'Is it a secret, this place?'

'Yes.'

Elf was looking out of the summer-house, horri-fied. Uncle Brownjohn had seen her. He was still smiling.

'That's the girl who was in the pantry. Aren't you going to introduce me?'

'She's Elf—Elfrida.'

Uncle Brownjohn went over to the summer-house and said something to Elfrida. Ben didn't know what. Then Uncle Brownjohn called across to him, 'Don't forget those eggs now!' and he looked back at his watch and saw it was time to fish them out. By the time he had done this, which was difficult, Uncle Brownjohn and Elf seemed to have made friends. Elf no longer looked horrified, more bemused. They came back to the fire together and

Elf said, 'You can have one of the eggs. We did two each. You can have two, if you like, and we'll have one each.'

'One will be enough,' said Uncle Brownjohn. 'We can toss for the extra one.'

Elf won the toss, so ate two while Ben and Uncle Brownjohn ate one each. Elf had brought him a deckchair and he sat eating without asking any questions.

All he said was, to Ben, 'Everyone's looking all over the place for you at home. We'll have to go back when we've finished.'

'How did you know I was here?' Ben asked.

'I saw the way you went.'

When he had finished his egg he said to Elfrida, 'Perhaps you would like to come back too, and stay with Ben?'

Elfrida didn't answer. Ben could see that she wanted to, just as she had been so pleased to come to breakfast the day before, but she was frightened. She finished her second egg, slowly.

'Do come,' Ben said, thinking of how he wouldn't have to worry about her so much. He wasn't used to all the worry he had been getting lately.

'I can't,' she muttered.

Uncle Brownjohn didn't say anything, except, 'Shall I help you wash up?'

They wiped the teaspoons clean and Uncle Brownjohn washed out the billy in the lake and they put the eggcups away in the summer-house.

'You'd better come along now, Jamineb, before they send out a search party.'

'All right.'

Ben sighed.

Elf stood at the summer-house door, looking all screwed up and suspiciously close to tears again.

'I'll come tomorrow,' Ben said.

'Goodbye then, Elfrida,' Uncle Brownjohn said politely. 'Thank you for the tea.'

'I'll come,' Elf said, very sharply. 'Will you wait while I shut the hens up?'

'Of course. Can we help?'

'It's too early, but I think they'll come,' Elf said.

She got some bread and opened the new pen (by lifting up the branches to make a hole) and carefully threw the breadcrumbs down in a trail to the summer-house. The hens pecked along it and they managed to round them in through the doors and shut them in.

'Very good,' said Uncle Brownjohn, full of admiration.

Elf smiled.

'There's a fox. He comes round. I've seen him.'

'I bet there are several.'

'I bet so too,' said Ben.

He felt fantastically happy to be going back home with both Uncle Brownjohn and Elf. Elf looked rather dirty, and he supposed he did too, but it didn't matter too much.

6

When they got back there was a great consternation and carry-on about where had he been and how worried they had been, and nobody seemed to be bothered about the extra Elfrida. Uncle Brownjohn said she was Ben's friend come to stay and his mother said vaguely, 'How nice, dear,' and that was all. Only Mitzi looked annoyed, and curious.

'Who is she?' she asked Ben.

'My friend.'

'She looks familiar. I must have seen her around somewhere.'

And she screwed her face up thoughtfully and

stared at Elf very hard. It was then that Ben remembered the poster and Mitzi eager for her thousand pounds, and all the worries that he had thought were over came back in a rush. Mitzi only had to fit Elf's face to the poster . . . ! She only had to remember.

However at the moment she was terribly busy trying to make scones for tea, and was using all her concentration so that they wouldn't come out like rocks as they usually did. By the time she remembered, Ben hoped very much to have off-loaded his problem on to Uncle Brownjohn.

'If you want to find your father, Uncle Brownjohn will help you,' he said to Elf at the first opportunity, which was when all the adults decided to watch a film on television in which some of them had acting parts. They all squashed round the television set with their drinks and cigarettes and talked and mimicked what was happening on the screen, and Ben and Elf sat in the kitchen eating chocolate biscuits. It was half past ten, long past their bedtime, but nobody seemed to bother. Even Mitzi was watching the film.

'Mitzi is going to remember that she saw your face on the poster. And she'll tell on you. She really wants a thousand pounds.'

Elf considered.

'I was going to go to the docks and meet my

father's ship,' Elf said. 'But when you said about the poster . . . it makes it difficult. There are always lots of police about in the docks.'

She took another chocolate biscuit out of the tin.

'I'm not really sure of the date the ship comes. I think it comes quite soon—Tuesday, I think. That's—that's why I came with you—here. I thought I could use your phone, to find out, if your mother wouldn't mind?'

'You can find out on the phone?'

'Lloyds know. You ring Lloyds.'

'Who are Lloyds?'

Elf frowned. 'I don't know. They're just people who tell you about ships.'

Ben thought it was a bank. A bank that knew about ships, perhaps.

'What if they say it's coming on Tuesday then?'

'I shall go.'

'How?'

'I don't know yet. On the train, I suppose, or a bus.'

She looked worried and perplexed, and Ben could see that the whole thing was very difficult. Especially when you were Wanted.

'It was all right before you told me about the poster,' she said crossly. 'But now I'm frightened to go anywhere. I'd have phoned and found out by now, if you hadn't said about the poster.'

She sounded accusing, as if he had messed it up for her.

To make amends, he said, 'Uncle Brownjohn will phone for you, I'm sure. He'll help you.'

Elf was obviously impressed by Ben's relations, probably because they didn't ask questions and fuss like ordinary relations. His mother hadn't even asked Elf where she had come from. 'Yes, do stay, darling,' she had said. 'How lovely for Ben to have a little friend.'

'Shall we ask him, when they've finished watching the film?'

'You're sure he won't tell on me?'

'No. He's not like that.'

'Nobody else though. Not the others.'

'No.'

The others all stuck with the television for hours, but at about eleven o'clock Uncle Brownjohn came out into the kitchen to get some water for his whisky. Ben was asleep with his arms across the table, and Elf had finished the chocolate biscuits and was looking in the fridge for something else.

'Hey, why aren't you two in bed?' Uncle Brownjohn was surprised.

'Nobody told us to go.'

'That figures,' he said. 'Shall I tell you?'

'Not yet,' Elf said.

Uncle Brownjohn filled his glass from the tap. He turned round and looked at her sternly.

'People are looking for you, you know. You are causing a lot of trouble.'

'Ben told you!'

'He did not. I figured it out for myself.'

He perched on the kitchen table and studied Elf with interest, not unkindly. She stared back at him defiantly.

'What are you going to do?' she asked him angrily.

'I would like to help you sort things out.'

'Tell the police? Tell my mother?'

'I didn't say that, did I?'

'I'm not doing anything wrong. Only waiting for my father to come home. My mother doesn't want me. She doesn't want my father anyway, but I want my father. I want my father!'

She looked angrier than Ben had ever seen her, but Ben was asleep. Uncle Brownjohn saw the tears glittering. He shook his head.

'What if I say, tomorrow I will help you? Tonight is too late. Go to bed and in the morning you can tell me what you want and I'll do my best to sort it out for you. But your little escapade has got to come to an end, you know that?'

Elf gave a great sigh, and the anger faded into a

patent weariness. It was more than being sleepy, Uncle Brownjohn recognized. But sleep would help. 'Sleep on it' was one of his mottoes.

He gave Ben a gentle shake.

'Come on, Jamineb. Bedtime.'

Ben opened his eyes.

'Have you rung Lloyds?'

'Lloyds are in bed,' said Uncle Brownjohn. 'As you should be.'

He saw them upstairs, and made a bed for Elf on Ben's floor with a pile of cushions that he collected up from all the rooms that had spare cushions and some blankets from other people's beds.

'There. And don't run away, because if you do, then I shall tell the police.'

She was asleep almost before he shut the door on them, and Ben supposed Uncle Brownjohn had taken over, and the relief engulfed Ben like warm bathwater, so that he felt back like a child again, instead of sixty. He slept so heavily he never heard anything until someone was shaking him quite violently, and he came awake very scared.

It was Elf. She was laughing.

'Come on, Skylark! Quick! Hurry! We're going to Felixstowe to meet my father!'

'When?'

'Now. Now, this minute! Hurry up!'

And she pulled all the covers off him.

'Now?!'

'Yes. Your uncle—he rang Lloyds and they said—they said the ship is there!—it came last night!—so hurry, hurry, you stupid Skylark, we're going now! Now!'

'Where's Uncle Brownjohn?'

'He's getting his car out of the garage.'

Elf threw Ben's vest at him.

'Hurry!'

She was all sort of shining and alight; he had never seen her look like that before.

'All those people have gone,' she said.

'What, my mother?'

He was scrambling into his clothes as fast as he could.

'I don't know about your mother. That Mitzi's still here. She keeps staring at me. Here's your sandals.'

She threw them at him. She kept bouncing up and down.

'Oh, stop it!'

'Hurry then!'

'I am hurrying!'

Elf ran out of the room, and Ben could hear a car revving up in the yard. He scrambled into his jersey anyhow and ran. Down the stairs and into the kitchen . . . the door was open.

Mitzi was sitting at the table with a cup of

coffee, her mouth wide open.

'That girl! She's the one on the poster! Ben, the Missing Person—she's the Missing Person, isn't she?'

Ben ran.

Mitzi made a grab at him but he twisted his arm out of her grip and fled. Mitzi got up and ran. Uncle Brownjohn was in his car with Elf sitting beside him and he was turning the car round to face the drive. He flung open the back door for Ben. Mitzi screamed after them, but one of her spiky heels stuck in a crack on the top of the kitchen steps and she came to an abrupt halt.

Ben leapt into the car, terrified.

'All right, Jamineb?'

He wasn't at all sure, but Uncle Brownjohn slammed the door and drove off down the drive. Ben turned round and saw Mitzi running after them with one shoe off and one shoe on, stumbling and waving, but as the drive curved round he lost sight of her. He felt relieved, but a bit guilty. Mitzi did need a thousand pounds, really. It was awful for her to miss it like that.

Elf was laughing, and still bouncing about.

'Fasten your seat-belt, child, and sit still,' Uncle Brownjohn said, rather severely.

'I'm hungry,' Ben said.

'It's gone ten o'clock, Jamboreen, you'll have to

wait till we get to Felixstowe. Elfrida and I have done a morning's work while you've been sleeping. That's what comes of not going to bed until someone tells you.'

'Mitzi usually tells me.'

'She was off-duty last night.'

'She's not this morning,' Elf said, and laughed. Then she stopped laughing and said, 'What if she tells?'

'What indeed?' said Uncle Brownjohn.

Ben couldn't be bothered to get worried again. The excitement of the day's beginning had made his head whirl, and he needed to sit and take in the peace and quiet of the passing countryside. He hoped Felixstowe wasn't far, because he was terribly hungry.

Having stopped bouncing, Elf was now wondering if Mitzi had rung up the police to apply for her thousand pounds.

'What if they're looking for me?'

'Put a blanket over your head,' Uncle Brownjohn suggested.

Ben was sitting on one which he passed over.

Elf arranged it over her head and sat quite still for a while, then said it was terribly hot. Ben could see only fields for miles in every direction.

'Why don't you just put it on for towns? No one's going to see you out here, only cows.'

Elf emerged, rather red in the face.

'How far is Felixstowe?' she asked.

'About forty miles.'

Forty miles to food! Ben felt weak. But Uncle Brownjohn had to stop for petrol and bought them some Mars bars and crisps and tins of drink, and after that Ben felt much better, and began to wonder what Elf's father was like. What the ship was like. What Felixstowe was like. He never went anywhere much, only sometimes to London, and otherwise just to the local town. Now the shocks were over he found he was quite enjoying himself. Perhaps, he thought, Elf's father would come and live with her in the summer-house. He must be nice, else she wouldn't want him so. He never much wanted his mother, he thought, although he was quite pleased to see her when she did turn up. But she never seemed to be there when he did want her, only when he didn't particularly, which meant you couldn't rely on her like he thought children were supposed to rely on mothers. He and Elf didn't seem to fit the rules.

As they approached Felixstowe Elf got under the blanket again, in spite of the fact that she looked rather more conspicuous under the blanket than not under the blanket.

'Like my old granny,' said Uncle Brownjohn.

But Elf preferred it that way, so missed their busy

threading through the traffic into the docks. Ben expected to see wide expanses of open sea, and liners, but it was all rather boring close-ups of lorries and sheds and notices, and the ships close to didn't look like ships somehow, more like blocks of flats or buildings in the course of being built. Uncle Brownjohn stopped to make enquiries—once off a policeman, which Ben thought very rash, but the policeman made no remark about the blanketed hump which was a thousand pounds' worth of Missing Person and so lost his opportunity for promotion and congratulation. This was very disappointing in Ben's eyes, although rather satisfactory otherwise.

Uncle Brownjohn parked the car and left them, to proceed on foot.

'It's going to be difficult. I might be a long time,' he said. 'Be patient.'

Elf lay down across the two front seats with the blanket over her.

'I feel a bit sick,' she said.

'It's those Mars bars.'

'No. It's my father.'

In spite of the blanket she kept shivering.

It was the longest wait Ben could ever remember—or felt like it, even if it wasn't. Nobody took any notice of them and Ben got hungrier and hungrier. Elf kept saying she felt sick. At last Uncle

Brownjohn came back. He opened the door on Elf's side and said, 'Out you get.'

She threw back the blanket and jumped out. Ben got out too.

'I can come too, can't I?'

'Yes, of course you can.'

Uncle Brownjohn then locked the car up and took them each by the hand and led them away at a great pace, through a lot of buildings and lorry parks and barriers and expanses of concrete, until they came to the side of a very large ship with two gangways going up into it. He stopped at the bottom of the first gangway.

'See anyone you know?' he said to Elf.

A man stood at the top of the gangway, dressed in overalls. He was too far away for Ben to make out exactly, but Elf gave a sort of scream and pulled herself out of Uncle Brownjohn's grasp and ran up the gangway. The man at the top came a few paces down to meet her, and they seemed to Ben to clash together, so that you couldn't tell one from the other, their arms tightly round each other. Then the man carried her up over the top and they disappeared into the ship.

Ben waited expectantly.

'So, that's it,' said Uncle Brownjohn, and took Ben's hand again. 'Come along.'

'I'm waiting for them!'

THIS WAY UP

THIS WAY UP

'You'll wait for ever, Jamineb.'

'What do you mean?'

'They don't want us any more.'

'Of course they do! Elf wants me!'

'Let's go and get something to eat.'

'And come back?'

'We'll have something to eat and see.'

He led Ben back to the car. Ben was so hungry he made no more protest, and Uncle Brownjohn drove the car out of the docks and stopped at a café on the roadside a short distance away. He locked up the car again and they went inside, into the steamy, fuggy atmosphere of beefburgers and hotdogs and chicken pie and chips. He let Ben choose whatever he wanted and bought a plateful for himself as well, and Ben chose a table by the window. So he could see Elf if she went by, he thought privately.

'I bet she's glad. I bet she's happy. We did her a good turn, didn't we?'

'I hope so,' said Uncle Brownjohn. 'It's what she wanted.'

'She'll tell us when she comes back. She'll tell us what he said. I bet he was surprised!'

'She won't come back.'

'She will. She's left all her things.'

The torch and the tin-opener and the hens and the china, the bucket and her sleeping-bag and the candles in the lemonade bottles.

'She will.'

'Jamboreen the Tambourine, she won't come back.'

Ben frowned. What did Uncle Brownjohn know about Elf?

'She doesn't want us any more,' he said. 'She has her father. I've told the police what's going on and they have been in touch with her mother, and the family is all going to get together and sort out their problems, and in that there is no room for us, Ben. We'll go home now. She knows where to find you, after all, doesn't she? If I'm wrong.'

Ben digested all this carefully.

'Will you get the thousand pounds then?'

Uncle Brownjohn laughed.

'No. I don't want a thousand pounds for doing that. They can keep it.'

Not Mitzi either. Poor Mitzi. Ben decided they might as well go home after all. He would try to explain it all to Mitzi.

'The hens will need feeding,' he remembered.

'Yes, that's right.'

7

They drove home, and Ben kept thinking of Elf flying up the gangway and the way her father hugged her. Nothing wrong with that, surely? But Uncle Brownjohn was very quiet and worried-looking, and did not say anything on the way home.

When they got back, the police were already there. Mitzi had called them after all. There were two of them drinking tea in the kitchen. Mitzi stood up and went very red when she saw Ben, as red as her shirt again, but Uncle Brownjohn said to her, 'It's all right, dear, you've done the right thing.'

She looked very relieved, and Ben knew how she felt, having been worried and relieved a lot himself recently.

Uncle Brownjohn told the police what he had done about Elf, and they seemed quite agreeable and wrote it all down in exercise books.

'A very headstrong child, apparently,' said one of the policemen. 'Her mother has a—er—lodger, to whom the girl has taken strong exception. They are rather feckless, but they do care, in their way.'

'She was amazingly resourceful, to live like that on her own for—how long?—four weeks? Six weeks?' Uncle Brownjohn said.

'Six weeks, about, sir. Perhaps we should see where she was hiding out before we go. Can you show us where it is?'

'Ben will show you,' said Uncle Brownjohn.

'Must I?'

'Yes, you must.'

So Ben led the way down to the summer-house and they all came—even Mitzi, staggering and tripping. Uncle Brownjohn took her arm, very gallant. The lake lay serene in the afternoon sun, and the hens were still shut in the summer-house from last night. Ben let them out, and they clucked and squawked crossly down to the lake for a drink. The cat lay on the roof, blinking. The policemen went into the summer-house and looked in all the drawers and discovered Elf's shiny possessions, and all the rows and rows of tinned food.

'Well, well, well,' they said.

'That's my bucket,' Mitzi said. 'That's why it kept coming and going.'

'I reckon this little girl departing will save us a lot of trouble,' one of the policemen said.

Uncle Brownjohn laughed.

'She never paid for any of it?'

'We've had a lot of complaints, this last six weeks. Shop-lifting. I reckon it all ended up here.'

Mitzi added, 'And George said he had lost two brown hens.'

They all looked round, impressed, almost admiring.

'Amazing,' said the policemen.

They wrote some more in the exercise books, then said they must go, and set off back for the house.

Ben said to Uncle Brownjohn, 'I'll feed the hens.'

'I must see the policemen off. Don't be long.'

They all departed. Ben fed the hens with Elf's bag of corn and then sat in the doorway of the summerhouse, working things out. It was very quiet without Elf, and sad, and lonely. It was like everything had been before he had discovered Elf. He did not believe she wouldn't come back. Uncle Brownjohn couldn't always be right.

He went slowly back through the wood, and sat by Oscar's grave. Even Oscar was a dead dog, after all. The dandelions were dead too. Uncle Brownjohn came back after the policemen had gone, and stood looking down on him.

'Eh up, Jamineb. What do we do next?'

'Nothing. There's nothing.'

'The fox'll get the hens again. I reckon we'll have to find them a home up here, so you can look after them.'

'Mitzi said they were George's hens.'

'George has been without them long enough. I reckon he would like you to have them now.'

'Would he, do you think?'

'I do think.'

Ben pulled the dead dandelions out of the jam jar and threw them in the rough grass.

'Oscar needs some more flowers too.'

He got up.

'Oscar came with me,' he said.

'We'll get Oscar some more flowers,' Uncle Brownjohn said, and put his arm round Ben.

Ben cheered up a bit looking for a new home for the hens by the house. Uncle Brownjohn said for now they could go in one of the old looseboxes in the stable, and they made them some nesting-boxes out of two old tea-chests, and found them a water-dish, and Uncle Brownjohn made them a perch.

'I hope we can catch them,' he said. He fetched a big cardboard box from the house to carry them in, and they went back to the summer-house to collect them. They laid a trail of corn into the summer-house and shut the doors on them when they were in, and Uncle Brownjohn managed to catch them with a lot of squawking and flying about, and swearing on his part. Ben closed the cardboard flaps down on the box.

'They're jolly heavy,' he said, testing.

They carried them back to their new home and when they were settled Ben and Uncle Brownjohn picked some more flowers for Oscar's grave.

'A dead dog's not much good,' Uncle Brownjohn said. 'Would you like a new one? A live one?'

'What, like Oscar?'

'Yes.'

'What, for me? A real dog?'

'Why not?'

Ben couldn't believe it. 'What will Mummy say?' She didn't like dogs. She said they were messy.

'She's gone. She won't know.'

They went in for tea, and Ben kept thinking about having a dog. Mitzi didn't like dogs either.

'I like dogs though,' said Uncle Brownjohn. 'And I'm going to stay here. It's a good place to work, here. Quiet. You and me, and a dog.'

'And Mitzi?'

'Mitzi doesn't like living here.'

'Her shoes are no good.'

'No, I've noticed.'

Uncle Brownjohn got the tea, as Mitzi seemed to have disappeared. Ben went upstairs and found her in her room, lying on the bed, crying. He went back and reported to Uncle Brownjohn.

'All those actors have upset her,' he said. 'I think she ought to get a job in films. She's the sort, she likes all that carry-on. Perhaps I could fix something up for her.'

Ben thought Mitzi would really like that. Even if she didn't get her thousand pounds, a job in films would make her happy.

'I'll fix something up for her, and I'll ask my housekeeper in London to come down here and do Mitzi's job. She's always wanting to live in the country. She's a farmer's daughter. She knows all about it, and wears the right shoes. She's not young and flighty like Mitzi, but old and sensible. She'd love it here.'

Uncle Brownjohn was warming to his theme, getting as excited as Ben.

'And you shall go to school and have lots of friends.'

'And a dog.'

'You shall choose a dog yourself. I'll take you to Battersea Dogs' Home and you shall choose the very dog you want.'

'Like Oscar.'

'Like Oscar. Oscar the second.'

'When?'

'Tomorrow.'

'Tomorrow! Can I tell Mitzi?'

'I'll tell Mitzi. We'll have a long chat.'

'What is Battersea Dogs' Home?'

'It's a great big kennels where they collect up all the stray dogs nobody wants. Then other people like us, who do want, go and choose one to take home.'

'If there was one for people, Elf could have gone.'

'Oh, Jamineb!'

For a moment Uncle Brownjohn lost all his

sparkle and looked very sad, but then Mitzi came down with a red nose and pink eyes and they started getting the tea. Somehow, everything felt quite different. Ben went to fetch the marmalade and when he stretched up his arm to the shelf he saw his bright yellow watch saying 16.46, and he thought of Elf, remembering her in the pantry, remembering her holding up the watch, laughing.

'When she comes back, I shall have a dog, a real dog called Oscar,' he said to himself.

And went to get his tea.